The Flying Toast

BBC CHiLDReN'S BOOKS

One day in Teletubbyland it was time for Tubby toast.

Laa-Laa pressed the button.

Tubby toast!

Tinky Winky smelled
something delicious.

Tinky Winky pressed the button.

Tubby toast!

The Tubby toaster began to make funny noises.

Dipsy and Po wondered what was going on.

There was Tubby toast all over the table.
There was Tubby toast all over the floor.

Uh~oh!

There was Tubby toast all over Tinky Winky.

There was Tubby toast everywhere.

There was lots of Tubby toast for Laa-Laa,
lots of Tubby toast for Dipsy,

Tubby toast!

lots of Tubby toast
for Tinky Winky,

Tubby toast!

lots of Tubby toast
for Po,

Tubby toast!

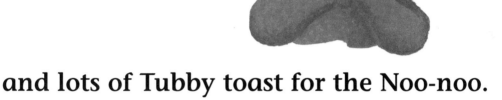

and lots of Tubby toast for the Noo-noo.

slurpy
sucky
sucky

Lots of Tubby toast
for everyone.

Teletubbies love Tubby toast, and
Teletubbies love each other very much.

Look out for the Teletubbies books, audio and video tapes.

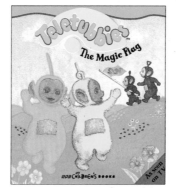

BBC CHiLDREN'S

First published in 1997 by BBC Children's Publishing, a division of BBC Worldwide Ltd
Woodlands, 80 Wood Lane, London W12 0TT

Adapted from the original script by Andrew Davenport
Illustrations by Lucy Su and Atholl McDonald. Text, design and illustrations copyright © 1997 BBC Children's Publishing
Teletubbies copyright © 1996 Ragdoll Productions (UK) Limited

ISBN 0 563 38050 0

Printed in Great Britain by Cambus Litho Ltd.